HOORAY for SNOW!

By Courtney Carbone
Illustrated by Zoe Waring

A GOLDEN BOOK • NEW YORK

PEPPA PIG and all related trademarks and characters TM & © 2003 Astley Baker Davies Ltd and/or Entertainment One UK Ltd. All rights reserved. Used with Permission. HASBRO and all related logos and trademarks TM & © 2021 Hasbro. Peppa Pig created by Mark Baker and Neville Astley.

www.peppapig.com

rhcbooks.com
Educators and librarians, for a variety of teaching tools, visit us at
RHTeachersLibrarians.com
ISBN 978-0-593-38053-6 (trade) — ISBN 978-0-593-38054-3 (ebook)
Printed in the United States of America   10 9 8 7 6 5 4 3 2 1

Peppa is so excited! There was a huge
snowstorm!

"Hooray!" Peppa and George exclaim
as they run down the stairs.

Daddy Pig is sitting by a small radio.
"No playgroup today," he reports.
"Yippee!" Peppa says. "Can we go outside?"
"Of course," Mummy Pig says. "Right after breakfast."

Peppa and George gobble down their pancakes,
then get dressed in their warmest clothes and boots.
"Don't forget your hats," Daddy Pig says. He is
wearing three hats at once!

Peppa and George laugh as they get ready.
"Daddy's taking us to the playground," Peppa says.
"Have fun!" Mummy Pig replies.

At the playground, everything is covered in snow.
Plop!
Peppa feels something hit her shoulder. She looks
up to see her friends—holding lots of snowballs!

"Look out, George!" Peppa says, running for cover.
She and George turn the merry-go-round into a
fort so they can make snowballs of their own.
Soon there are snowballs flying everywhere.

Peppa and her friends stop throwing
snowballs when they see Rebecca and
Richard Rabbit with brand-new sleds.
They all take turns racing down the hill.
Everyone wants to try to be the fastest.

"Whee!"

After sledding, Peppa
decides to build a snow pig.

Peppa's friends want to build snow creatures of their own.

Soon, the playground is filled with a snow dog, a snow rabbit, a snow zebra, a snow elephant, a snow sheep, a snow pony, a snow cat, and a tiny snow dinosaur!

Peppa plops down in the snow.

She moves her arms up and down.
She moves her legs back and forth.
Peppa has made a snow angel.

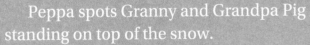

Peppa spots Granny and Grandpa Pig standing on top of the snow.

"Your shoes look like tennis rackets!" Peppa tells them.

Granny and Grandpa Pig laugh.

"These are called snowshoes," Granny Pig explains. "They keep us from sinking into the snow."

Granny and Grandpa Pig are going skating at the ice rink.

"Would you like to come along?" Granny Pig asks. "We stopped by the house to get your ice skates."

She holds up a lumpy sack, and Peppa and George cheer.

At the skating rink, Peppa recognizes lots of friends
from around town. She sees Mrs. Zebra, Miss Rabbit,
and even her teacher, Madame Gazelle!
Peppa waves hello as she laces up her skates.

Ice-skating isn't easy, but it sure is fun!
Grandpa Pig skates in long, winding curves.

Granny Pig skates in
fancy figure eights.

George does all sorts of moves, but his tracks just look like squiggles.

They are all having so much fun that no one notices the sun going down.

Granny Pig looks at her watch. "Time to head home," she says.

Peppa says goodbye to her friends. She doesn't want the fun to end, but she must admit that she is starting to get hungry.

Back at her house, Peppa sees
that the snow has started to melt.
This gives her an idea for one last
snow day activity!

Splash!
She jumps into a mushy, slushy puddle.
Splash! Splash! Splash!
George is quick to join in the fun.

Peppa and George go inside and take off their slushy, wet boots. The day is done, but there is still one more treat in store.

"Surprise!" Mummy Pig announces.
She and Daddy Pig have made
gingerbread cookies and mugs of
steaming hot chocolate for everyone.
Peppa and George give a loud cheer.
But Grandpa Pig cheers the loudest of all!

Peppa and George snuggle under a
blanket with their mugs of hot chocolate.
What a wonderful day it has been!
"Hooray for snow!" says Peppa.